Catching Air!

Story by Julie Ellis
Illustrations by Mini Goss

Contents

Chapter 1

The Basics

"Bad luck, Becks. You really packed into the snow that time," a voice called loudly. "Pull yourself up by the toe of your board."

Rebecca spat out a mouthful of snow, adjusted her goggles, and glared angrily at her snowboard, ignoring her cousin John's comment. They had both started snowboarding lessons three days ago, but already John was trying to give her advice.

Snowboarding wasn't easy, but Rebecca wasn't about to give up. Besides, it had taken ages to persuade her mother to let her have snowboarding lessons.

Despite feeling like a blob in the chunky boots, snow pants, and thickly padded gloves, Rebecca managed to roll onto her knees and stand up. Now, if she could just learn to stay up!

Looking down the hill she could see John practicing an *ollie*. He looked quite stylish, jumping up, catching air, using his arms to balance himself.

Trying to remember what their instructor, Petra, had told them, Rebecca boarded after John as fast as she dared. She kept her knees bent and her weight over the middle of the board, but her arms still waved about as she tried to keep her balance.

John was waiting for Rebecca at the end of the line for the chairlift.

"Hurry up, Becky. I want to try a few tricks. By the end of this week I want to be able to do a perfect *grab*."

"Okay, okay," replied Rebecca. John kept hassling her to keep up with him. Rebecca just wanted to go at her own pace.

As they inched their way toward the chairlift, Rebecca began to feel panicky. Getting on and off the lift was supposed to be easy, but she worried about missing the chair, or catching her board on the ground as she sat.

When it was their turn to get on, Rebecca slid into the pick-up space, with John beside her. She watched over her shoulder as the chair came closer. Then she grabbed the handrail and sat down. Just in time, she remembered to lift the toe of her board off the ground.

Now Rebecca could relax and listen to what John was saying. He was pointing to a group of people below them.

"Look! That must be the film crew your mom said she'd seen," he said. "I heard they're making a documentary about snowboarding. Wouldn't it be cool if they filmed me?"

"In your dreams!" laughed Rebecca. Leaning over the safety bar, she felt relaxed and happy.

It was a beautiful day. The air was clear, the sun was warm, and the snow was glinting brilliantly. There was laughter on the slope below them as people got down the mountain in a variety of ways.

All too soon, Rebecca realized that they were approaching the end of the ride. Getting off the chair would be even trickier than getting on.

"Don't fall off this time," she whispered to herself. Then she lifted the safety bar over her head just as the lift approached the ramp.

Rebecca had fallen off every time so far. She swallowed hard and gripped the seat to stop her hands from shaking.

She tried to copy what John was doing. As he moved forward, leaned over, and stood up, she did the same. To her complete surprise, she found herself gliding smoothly down the off ramp.

Rebecca couldn't stop grinning.

"It's so simple," she thought. "All I have to remember is to stand up before trying to ride away."

Chapter 2

The Attack

Feeling more confident, Rebecca boarded quickly after John, who turned and called out, "Let's find some bumps. I want to practice jumps. You can be my spotter."

"Well, I want to practice jumps too, so we'll take turns being spotter," Rebecca yelled back.

John had seen the film crew. He headed over to some bumps that were within their view.

Rebecca boarded past some bumps and stopped below them. She waved at John when the area was clear of people.

John sped into the bumps. He worked hard on his jumps. He was careful to take off and land with his board flat, but while he was airborne he practiced grabs.

First he did a *mute*, grabbing the toe-side edge of his board. Then he tried the more difficult *indy*, reaching his back hand behind his feet, to again grab the toe-side of his board. Finally he did some tail grabs.

"How did I look?" he asked casually, as he slid to a stop beside Rebecca.

"Not bad," Rebecca laughed. "Unfortunately the film crew didn't notice you."

"Well, it's your turn now. I'll be your spotter," replied John, and he slid further down the hill.

As Rebecca looked at the bumps, she felt a familiar tightness in her chest, and she suddenly found it hard to breathe. Oh no, not an asthma attack — not now!

Rebecca patted her pants and jacket, trying to find her inhaler. She felt a lump in her jacket pocket. She pulled off her gloves, unzipped the pocket and found a chocolate bar. She needed her inhaler, but where was it?

Rebecca sat down and tried to concentrate on breathing and relaxing. She was beginning to wheeze. She could hear John calling out to her, "Come on! Hurry up!"

Looking down the slope, Rebecca saw him climbing back up to her. She could tell from his body language that he was annoyed. However, as soon as he reached her, he could hear her wheezing and he realized she was having an asthma attack.

"Where's your inhaler?" he asked.

"In the car," Rebecca whispered breathlessly, and pointed to the distant parking lot that was full of tiny cars.

"I'll get it for you," said John, suddenly becoming decisive. "But I'll have to find your mom to get the car keys."

He looked around him at the hundreds of brightly colored people on the ski field.

"How will I find her?" he asked. "She could be anywhere."

Summoning all her strength, Rebecca wheezed, "Tell the office. They'll radio the lift operators."

John understood. At the top of each chairlift was a message board. The office staff could radio messages up to the lift operators, who would then write them on the board. John could get a message to Rebecca's mother.

"It's going to take me a while to get your inhaler," said John anxiously, "and I don't want to leave you alone."

John looked around him. Further down the slope, he could see someone wearing a bright purple jacket with red trim on it.

"I think I can see Petra," he told Rebecca. "I'll ask if she can come and sit with you while I get your inhaler."

Clipping his board back on, he raced as fast as he could after the purple jacket. As he got closer, he could see it really was Petra.

Quickly, John told Petra about Rebecca's asthma attack. She agreed to go and sit with Rebecca.

Rebecca tried to relax as she waited, but it was difficult to breathe. The cold mountain air was making her chest hurt. She hunched down with her face inside her jacket, feeling very alone. She hoped John would hurry.

Chapter 3

Petra's News

Rebecca heard someone calling her name. She struggled to her feet and saw Petra making her way up the slope. She immediately felt better, knowing she had company, and sat down again on the slope after Petra had reached her.

Petra sat down beside Rebecca. "Are you okay? Would a drink of water help?" she asked.

Rebecca shook her head. She felt too breathless to speak, or to drink.

Petra rubbed Rebecca's back and started talking to her. She said something about a snowboarding competition. But Rebecca was concentrating on her breathing, so she didn't really listen to what Petra was saying.

John soon arrived back with Rebecca's worried mother.

"Rebecca, are you okay?" she asked. "Here's your inhaler. Try to breathe slowly. We'll sit here with you while you recover."

Feeling relieved, Rebecca used her inhaler and slowly got her breath back.

As Rebecca was recovering, Petra repeated her news to John. "There's a *halfpipe* competition on Thursday," she told him. "You could enter the novice class. It's for people in their first season of boarding."

Smiling at Rebecca, she added, "So could Rebecca if she's feeling up to it."

John looked delighted with the news. Rebecca felt disappointed.

"I'm not a good enough boarder," she thought. "I'd probably stress out. I'll never keep up with John now."

John turned to Rebecca and her mother. "What do you think?" he asked. "Should we give it a try?"

Rebecca forced a smile. "You go for it," she replied. "I'm not good enough to enter yet, but I'll come and cheer you on."

"I'm glad you're being so sensible," Rebecca's mother smiled at her. "We don't want you to have another asthma attack. You can come and ski with me. Leave the boarding to John."

John grinned at Rebecca, "I'll show you how it's done."

Chapter 4

Rebecca's Plan

Suddenly Rebecca remembered why she'd taken up snowboarding.

It was the challenge.

Skiing with her mother was okay, but learning to board with John was lots more exciting. Rebecca felt angry with herself. She was giving up too easily.

"I'll enter the competition secretly and surprise both Mom and John," she thought. "I still have a day and a half to practice."

Feeling better, she boarded down to the lodge for lunch with the others.

Rebecca had an idea. She'd ask Petra for some hints.

After their Wednesday morning lesson, Rebecca managed to have a quick word with Petra while John was busy practicing more ollies.

Petra briefly explained the competition. "You have to enter the pipe at the top, do whatever tricks you can on your way down, and exit the pipe at the bottom without falling off. You're allowed to have two practice runs first."

Petra also loaned Rebecca a booklet called *Pipe Tricks*.

For the rest of the day, Rebecca practiced the easiest of the airborne grabs. By the end of the day, she could grab the tip of her board with her front hand, and with her back hand. Rebecca was catching air and she felt elated.

Rebecca didn't see John. He was busy practicing his own tricks, and trying to keep within sight of the film crew. He had high hopes of being filmed.

That evening John talked excitedly about the next day's competition. The film crew was intending to get some footage, and John wanted to be on it.

Rebecca felt panic rising within her.

"What if I crash?" she thought. "Imagine if the film crew films me doing a *face-plant!* I should just forget the whole idea and save myself the embarrassment."

On Thursday though, Rebecca felt more optimistic. She had the morning to practice because the competition wasn't until the afternoon. She spent some time practicing grabs on a ridge, and then, feeling more confident, she boarded over to the halfpipe.

Looking into the halfpipe, Rebecca saw that the snow was packed very hard.

"If I fall on that it will be like falling onto concrete," she thought.

Chapter 5

Wipeout!

During her first practice run down the halfpipe, Rebecca just concentrated on getting to the exit without falling.

On her second run, she tentatively tried a grab. Crouching down low over her board, she sped up the side of the pipe. As she became airborne, she reached her front hand down to grab her board. Unexpectedly, the board tilted. She lost her balance, plunging down the side of the pipe, and finally hitting the ground hard.

"Ouch, ouch, ouch!" she thought, as tears of pain and frustration welled. "I hate this. It's too hard. I'm not entering this silly competition."

Rebecca caught up with John after lunch.

"I've got a great routine worked out," he told her excitedly. "I've been practicing like mad. I'm going to do some grabs, and then halfway down the pipe I'm going to do a *hand-plant* on the side of the wall."

"I'd better come and watch then," answered Rebecca, feeling a little envious.

"Good luck!" she called to John, as he walked up the track to wait with the other novice boarders at the top of the halfpipe. The film crew was in position near the edge of the pipe, about halfway down. Rebecca moved down the hill so that she could watch John's ride.

When it was John's turn, he shot across the pipe — managing to keep his balance — and performed an indy, followed by a tail grab.

As he neared the film crew, he prepared to hand-plant. He approached the wall quickly, went up the side, planted his hands against the wall, and straightened his arms. Then he swung his legs up and tried to stall himself with his legs above his body.

He was going too fast. The momentum swung his board over. He tipped over and crashed out of Rebecca's sight down the sidewall.

A moment later, Rebecca saw him sliding into view. His body stopped and he lay still, face down in the bottom of the pipe.

Rebecca stared at his still body.

Slowly John began to move. He pushed himself onto his hands and knees, and then stood up on his board. There was blood running down his face.

He began boarding down to the exit, grinning rather gingerly at the clapping, whistling spectators.

Rebecca felt ill. She definitely didn't want to attempt a halfpipe ride now.

Chapter 6

The Challenge

"Rebecca, it's nearly your turn," shouted Petra, beckoning Rebecca up to the start.

Rebecca shook her head. "No, I'm not doing it," she called back.

Petra walked down to Rebecca.

"Did John's fall scare you?" she asked. "He fell because he was over-confident. You're not John. Face this challenge, but go carefully, and you'll enjoy it."

As Petra talked, Rebecca realized she had been trying too hard. She would take a turn, and do her best. She walked over to join the line.

When it was her turn, Rebecca headed slowly down the pipe, concentrating on keeping her board flat. She didn't attempt any jumps. All she wanted to do was to get down the halfpipe without falling.

As she traversed carefully down the pipe, Rebecca felt her confidence building.

"I can do this," she thought. "It's really happening."

She zigzagged neatly down the pipe and straight through the exit. She felt fantastic. She had boarded the halfpipe without falling!

She walked over to John, who was holding a tissue over a cut on his forehead.

"I didn't know you'd entered," he said. "You made it down without falling. Great job! Should we hang around for the awards?"

Rebecca laughed. "You never know your luck, John."

Chapter 7

Rewarded

There were quite a few awards handed out. "The Most Falls," "The Highest Jump," "The Most Flamboyant," "The Fastest." John won an award for "The Most Spectacular Crash."

To Rebecca's surprise, she also won an award — "The Most Controlled." Secretly she was rather pleased. That would impress her mother, and hopefully shut John up.

John, however, was feeling quite pleased with himself. He even approached the film crew to see if they had filmed him.

"You must be the kid who cartwheeled and then face-planted," said the guy with the camera, looking at John's battered face.

John smiled, pleased to be recognized.

"Yes, we got you. You're a good example of what happens when you lose control in a halfpipe," the man continued. "You're lucky you didn't break something."

John looked ruefully at Rebecca. She laughed as she walked away. "Well, you got your wish. You wanted to be filmed, and you were," she smiled.

Glossary

face-plant	crashing into the snow, face first
grab	reaching back or forward to grab the rear (tail) or front of the board
halfpipe	a ramp shaped like a U; snowboarders ride up the sides of the halfpipe, jumping out and doing tricks
hand-plant	planting the front or rear hand on the wall of the halfpipe while the body rotates
indy	using the back hand to grab the toe-side edge of the board
mute	holding the toe-side edge of your board with the front hand
ollie	jumping a board off flat land